Arlene Phillips OBE is a world-renowned director and choreographer creating musicals, videos, films, television programming and spectaculars. Her inventive choreography has been seen in the musicals *Grease, We Will Rock You, Starlight Express, The Sound of Music, Flashdance* and *The Wizard of Oz*. Her screen work includes the films *Annie* and *Legend*, and the television shows *DanceX* and *Britannia High*. Arlene's videos have starred everyone from Robbie Williams to Elton John, Whitney Houston to Tina Turner. Her largest ever spectacular was the XVII Commonwealth Games. She is known throughout the UK as a former judge on *Strictly Come Dancing* and now on *So You Think You Can Dance?* Her favourite job, however, has been as mother to her two daughters, Alana and Abi.

First published in 2010
by Faber and Faber Limited
Bloomsbury House
74–77 Great Russell Street
London WC1B 3DA

Typeset by Baobab Editorial and Design
Printed in England by Bookmarque, Croydon, UK

With thanks to Susan Reuben

The right of Arlene Phillips to be identified as author of this work
has been asserted in accordance with Section 77 of the Copyright,
Designs and Patents Act 1988

A CIP record for this book
is available from the British Library

978–0–571–25989–2

2 4 6 8 10 9 7 5 3 1

Samba Spectacular

By Arlene Phillips

Illustrated by Pixie Potts

faber and faber

Miss Trina

Keisha

Matthew

Verity

The Students at Step Out Studio

Alana

Meena

Chloe

Toby

*For Abi, who has always
inspired me*

Chapter 1

'Alana can't da-ance! Alana can't
da-ance!'

Alana spun round to find out where
the mocking voice was coming from,
nearly falling over on her samba heels.

Then she spotted her little sister,
peeping through the crack in her
bedroom door. 'Abi!' she shouted.

Alana had been trying and trying
to get the samba routine right for

her dance show the coming weekend, and the more she practised, the more mistakes she made. Now Abi the Annoying was making things even worse by laughing at her.

'Ouch!' Abi shrieked as the swinging door whacked her on the forehead. 'Mum! Mum!' she screamed. 'Alana hit me with the door!'

'I didn't do it on purpose!' yelled Alana. 'And you shouldn't have been hiding behind it spying on me, should you?'

'Girls, can you *please* be quiet?' came a weary voice from down the stairs. 'I've just done a twelve-hour shift at the restaurant and I've got a splitting headache. All I want is five minutes' peace.'

'But, Mum, I thought you were making

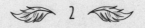 2

my dress for the show,' Alana said.

'Oh, Alana, I completely forgot about it. I'm sorry.'

Alana couldn't believe it. The show was being given by her dance school, Step Out Studio. It was called 'Latin Spectacular'. Alana and her mum had gone out at the weekend and bought this fantastic sea-green material and her mum was meant to be making it into a samba dress. How could she have forgotten? Surely she knew how important dancing was to her?

Alana sat down at the top of the stairs with her head in her hands. 'It's too late now to make the dress before the show, isn't it?' she asked, trying to keep the quiver out of her voice.

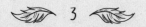 3

'It certainly is,' said Mum. 'I've got to spend this evening studying for my computing diploma and I'm working all day tomorrow.'

'Well can we go out now and *buy* a dress then? One of those ready-made ones? Pleeeease!' begged Alana.

'How do you imagine we can afford to do that?' asked Mum, losing patience. 'Honestly, Alana, you'd think that your silly dancing was the only thing that mattered. Here am I trying to look after you and Abi

and working all hours, and you can only think about samba frocks and tango steps, jazz moves and ballet positions. Shouldn't you be concentrating on more important things, like helping me out round here? Perhaps it's time you gave up dance classes!'

'I already spend half my time looking after Abi,' Alana muttered, but she didn't dare say it loud enough for her mum to hear. Instead, she went back into her bedroom, slammed the door and threw herself on the bed to have a good cry. Surely, surely Mum wouldn't make her give up dancing?

Once she had calmed down a bit, she rolled on to her back and gazed around her room. This always made her feel better. Her bedroom was her peaceful

hideout. Above her bed was a gigantic
poster of Darcey Bussell in *Swan Lake*, and
covering her walls were pictures of every
possible kind of dancing. There was her
favourite band TJS doing a dance move
from their latest song, another one of
Vincent and Flavia doing the tango, and
a poster from when she'd been to see the

musical of *Billy Elliot*.

Alana's room wasn't that big, but she
still managed to do dance practice in it.
Long ago she'd taken her carpet away
so that she had a hard floor to dance on.
The floorboards were a bit scuffed and
they were uneven in places, but it was
still a lot better than nothing.

Alana rolled over to her side and propped herself up on one elbow. On a shelf next to her bed, neatly lined up, were the cups and trophies that she'd won in dance competitions, and on the wall above them were framed certificates from all her dancing exams. She'd been going in for them ever since she was four. On her chest of drawers was a beautiful Spanish flamenco fan that she'd found in a market, and on the back of the door was a giant shoe rack to hold her ballet shoes, tap shoes, jazz and samba shoes. These were mostly second-hand, because new dance shoes were far too expensive.

Alana picked up her best treasure. It was a jewellery box her auntie had brought back from Austria. It was covered in pink silk and silver sequins. When you wound it up and opened the lid, two miniature ballroom dancers waltzed round and round. Alana watched them spin and drifted off into her own private dancing dream world. Just then, there was a timid knock on the door.

'Who is it?' called Alana.

'Oh, it's you,' she said, as Abi's rosy-cheeked face peeped around the door. 'Have you come to laugh some more?'

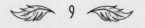

'I've come to say sorry,' replied Abi. 'I think it's rubbish that you're not going to have a samba dress for your show. And I really hope Mum doesn't make you give up dancing cos I know it's your favourite thing.'

'Thanks, Abs,' said Alana, patting the bed beside her. Abi came and sat down and nestled her head against Alana's shoulder. Alana put her arm around her. She has her good points, she thought grudgingly. Just then, the doorbell rang, and Alana ran downstairs to answer it. It was her best friend Meena and her dad, come to give her a lift to Step Out Studio to rehearse for the show. Alana practically flew out of the door, shouting goodbye to Mum and Abi as she went.

'What's the matter?' asked Meena, as Alana got into the car. 'You look like you've been crying.' Meena was whispering so her dad wouldn't hear.

Alana could always tell Meena anything. 'It's Mum, as usual,' she said. 'She's forgotten to make my samba dress, and even worse, she says maybe I've got to give up dancing altogether!'

'Oh no! That's terrible!' said Meena sympathetically.

'I'm going to look so stupid at the show tomorrow, dancing in my leotard and old black skirt. Especially when snotty Verity will probably have had her costume hand-made for her by some posh dress designer!'

'But it's the dancing itself that matters,' said Meena.

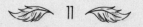

'Well, that makes it even worse!' replied Alana. I've been practising the samba routine in my room for hours, and I just can't get all the rhythm changes. I don't know what's the matter with me!'

But there wasn't time for any more moaning, because just then, Meena's dad pulled up outside Step Out Studio. 'Off you go girls – have a lovely time!' he said. He had no idea of the drama that had been going on in the back seat!

Chapter 2

As soon as Alana and Meena entered the practice room, they were hit by a torrent of noise. The dance students were excited about the show and they were all chatting madly. The girls ran over and joined in, starting their warm-up exercises as they talked.

But suddenly everyone fell quiet when a girl with wavy hair exploded into the room, tripping over as she went and

sliding all the way across the floor to land
at the feet of a tall, thin girl.

'Oh gosh, sorry, clumsy me!' said the
new girl, going bright red and giggling
like mad. 'I'm Chloe, by the way.'

'I'm Verity,' the tall girl replied, looking
at Chloe as if she were something she'd
just trodden in by accident.

'Ooh, isn't your dress pretty,' said
Chloe, looking at Verity's beautiful
orange and gold samba dress. 'It's almost
as pretty as you!'

But Verity didn't bother to reply. She'd
already turned away and started talking
to a dark-haired boy. The boy looked
a bit uncomfortable, and shrugged
apologetically at Chloe.

Alana came over to Chloe and helped

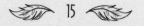

her up. She was about to say something comforting about how Verity was always nasty, when she realised that Chloe was still grinning from ear to ear. She didn't even seem to have noticed Verity had been rude.

So Alana offered to show Chloe around, before the class started.

Chloe gazed around her, taking in the big studio with its shiny floor of dark wood, and full-length mirrors lining the walls. Alana pointed out the barre that was used for ballet classes. Then they set off to look at the rest of the building.

'Isn't Verity beautiful!' said Chloe as they walked out of the main rehearsal room. Alana just shrugged, but didn't say anything.

'And who was that gorgeous boy with dark hair she was with?' continued Chloe.

'Oh, that's Matthew,' said Alana, with more enthusiasm. He's the best boy dancer we've got. Verity always manages to be his partner, unfortunately.'

Alana showed Chloe the props cupboard, which was crammed full of everything imaginable for all types of

dance: ribbons and feather boas, canes and top hats, skipping ropes and garlands of artificial flowers.

Chloe just stood there, looking at all the things in astonishment. 'Come on!' said Alana. She took Chloe by the arm and pulled her gently away, closing the props cupboard behind her. 'I'll show you the changing rooms.

'Everyone gets their own locker,' she explained. Then she pointed to one at the end of the row. 'This one's empty,' she said. 'Why don't you take it?' As Chloe was hanging up her coat in her locker, she asked what the dance teacher Miss Trina was like.

'She's strict,' Alana replied. 'She hates it if you don't try your hardest, but she's

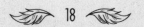

properly nice underneath it all. I like her loads. And she always looks ultra glam!'

'Yes,' sighed Chloe. 'I met her when I came for my audition. I wish I was as beautiful as her.'

'Let's go,' said Alana. 'We'd better get back to the rehearsal room – we'll be starting in a minute.'

As they passed near Verity, Alana heard her whisper to one of the other girls, 'Have you heard – there's a new girl called Marshmallow?'

Alana flushed with anger and looked at Chloe, but Chloe didn't seem to have heard.

Just then, there was a sharp clap, clap, clap! and at once everyone fell silent. Miss Trina was standing at the front waiting

to begin. She was as stylish as always, with her silky blonde hair parted in the middle and tied back in a ponytail. She was wearing a black cashmere cross-over cardigan and an elegant black samba skirt 'Now, students,' she said, 'this is our last rehearsal before the Spectacular, so I want everyone to concentrate hard, and *no mistakes*!' Her face softened slightly, as she continued, 'Remember everyone, the samba is the dance of Brazil, the dance of the Carnival, so I want to see you all giving it real energy and the wow factor! It's Carnival time!'

Alana was paired up with Toby. At eleven, he was the same age as Alana and he'd been coming to Step Out Studio for longer. But he hated it. He would much rather be out skateboarding with his mates and he thought dancing was totally uncool.

Alana just couldn't get the complicated samba rhythms right this evening. 'Come on, girls, use the hips!' called Miss Trina. 'Let your feet do the talking! Promenade into turning voltas!' But Alana's mind was elsewhere. She was thinking about the costume material waiting at home that was never going to get sewn, and – much worse – her mum's comment about her giving up dancing altogether.

Toby wasn't even trying. He had a grumpy expression the whole time and he was practically  just walking the steps, which made it even harder for Alana to get the bounce action she needed.

Toby's mum had been a professional dancer till she'd injured her knee and couldn't continue. So she was determined that someone in her family should dance if it couldn't be her. She didn't stop to think about whether that was what Toby wanted.

I feel sorry for Toby for having to come

here when he doesn't want to, Alana
thought. But at least he could try a bit
harder to lead me, for my sake. But she
knew that Toby would rather be dancing
with Meena. It was only when those two
paired up that Toby started making a bit
of an effort.

As the students were getting their coats
on after the class, Miss Trina drew Alana
to one side. 'What's going on, Alana?' she
asked, sternly, but her eyes were kind. 'You
were all over the place this evening.'

Alana didn't feel like talking about it.
'I'm just tired, I suppose,' she mumbled.
'Anyway – gotta go. Meena's dad's
waiting for me.' And she dashed out the
door before Miss Trina had a chance to
say anything else.

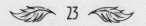
23

Chapter 3

The next day, Alana walked to school in a dream. Abi was scampering by her side, talking non-stop, but Alana just answered 'yes' and 'no' automatically without actually listening. 'Even if Mum lets me carry on dancing,' she thought, 'maybe Miss Trina won't want me in her classes any more if I dance in the show as badly as I did at rehearsal yesterday.'

Miss Trina let Alana come to Step Out

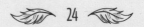

Studio for free. Her mum couldn't afford to send her otherwise, and Miss Trina thought she was talented enough to have a place. But Alana was always worrying that she'd change her mind.

Alana was thinking and worrying so much that she wasn't even looking where she was going. She suddenly crashed headlong into a tall, auburn-haired girl walking the other way with a gang of

friends. 'Sorry!' she gasped. Then she saw who she'd bumped into. It was Verity. Verity was in her posh uniform for Primula Prep School – a green and purple checked tunic, green tights, purple tie, green and purple striped blazer and green corduroy beret.

'This is the girl I was telling you about!' Verity screeched to her friends. 'The one whose mum can't afford to pay for her dance classes. And she's so clumsy she can't even walk straight down the pavement, never mind do a dance routine!' The other girls sniggered.

All at once, Verity found herself
head-butted by a small, furious
creature. It was Abi! Verity squealed in

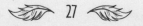

shock, as Abi began to shout at her.

'Don't you dare talk to my sister like that, snot face!' she yelled. 'I bet she can dance a million times better than you! *And* our mum's got loads of money, but she's keeping it so she can take us all to Disneyland, so there!'

The Primula Prep girls started laughing even harder now.

'Abi!' begged Alana, dragging her off. 'Come on! We're going to be late for school!'

'I was only trying to help!' said Abi as they walked away.

'I know,' said Alana. 'And it was sweet of you to stick up for me. But Verity is just going to be even worse now. Funny — you'd think she'd be too embarrassed about having to wear that silly uniform to be so nasty.'

Alana's day didn't improve when she got to Rosebury Primary. It was science followed by maths, and they were her worst subjects. She tried her best to concentrate, but she just kept doodling and staring out the window. Mrs Bailey the maths teacher was OK so long as you tried hard, but she hated it when her pupils didn't listen.

'Alana!' she said, rapping on her desk and making her jump. 'I see that you've been writing down the answer to the problem I've set you. Let me have a look.' She picked up Alana's exercise book, but the only thing on the page were sketches of dancers doing different samba steps.

Mrs Bailey raised her eyebrows. 'Perhaps,' she said, 'if I show your book to the whole class, they will be able to see your excellent maths work.' She held Alana's exercise book high, and everyone started to giggle as they saw the page covered in drawings. Only Meena, who was sitting next to her, didn't laugh. She squeezed Alana's hand under the

desk as Alana flushed bright red with embarrassment.

Things didn't get any better after lunch when they went outside to play netball. Alana was very fit from all her dance training, but she didn't have a good eye for the ball. She was playing Goal Attack, and she didn't manage to get the ball in the net once.

The best person in her class at sport was Keisha, who also went to Step Out Studio. Keisha was tall and strong, and she was head of the school netball team.

'Sorry, Keisha, I was rubbish today,' said Alana as they were getting changed out of their sports kit.

'Hmmm, well you're certainly not going to be my first choice for the netball team!'

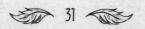

laughed Keisha, dragging off her trainers.

'It's a good job!' Alana replied. 'It's hard enough getting my mum to let me dance after school. There's no way I'd be able to do anything else as well.'

'If I had to choose between Step Out Studio and playing netball,' said Keisha, 'I'd definitely pick netball.'

'Are you kidding?' Alana replied. 'I'd choose dancing every time!'

Alana was relieved when the day was over at last and she could go home. As she walked down the high street, she gazed absently at the familiar shops. She smiled and waved at the man behind the counter in the newsagent's – she always went in there for dance magazines if she'd managed to save up enough pocket money. Her smile faded, though, when she'd gone past. Everything seemed so dreary – the street was smelly with traffic fumes and crowded with stressed-out shoppers; the air was damp, and icy gusts of wind kept blasting their way through her jacket; and all the time, the memory hung over her of her mum saying she might have to give up dancing.

Then, just as she was turning the corner on to her own road, she noticed a shop she'd never seen before. The name above the door read 'Madame Coco's Costume Emporium'. The sign was faded as though the shop had been there for years.

That's so weird, thought Alana. How can there be a costume shop at the end of my street that I've never even noticed!

You couldn't see through the window what was inside because it was draped in richly coloured cloths. All that Alana could make out was a strange glow, that didn't seem quite like a normal electric light. She just had to have a closer look!

Chapter 4

Alana pushed open the shop door
nervously, the hinges creaking. As soon as
she stepped inside, she was overwhelmed
by a tall lady wearing a sparkly shawl,
very high heels and a great deal of
make-up.

'Welcome, ma petite!' cried the lady,
giving Alana a huge hug. Alana didn't
know what to think. This sort of thing
didn't usually happen when she went into

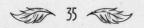

the local shops!

'I am Madame Coco!' the lady continued. 'And you are . . . ?'

'Er . . . Alana,' Alana replied.

'And I see you are a dancer!' Madame Coco continued.

'How did you know?' asked Alana in surprise.

'Ah, you just have that look about you, ma petite. I can always tell. I have dressed all the best dancers, you know. Ooh-la-la the stories I could tell you! Why, there was the case of the famous prima ballerina's tutu ... Oh but I am talking too much, ma chérie, and you haven't even had a chance to look round my shop.'

Alana's eyes grew wide as she gazed around her. In front of her were rail after rail of the most incredible dance costumes. There were tutus, glittering ballgowns, character costumes and salsa dresses. Stretching up to the ceiling were shelf after shelf crammed with feather boas, rolls of ribbon, bags of sequins and rhinestones, fans and masks, and every type of dance shoe you could think of. Alana wandered around gently touching the gorgeous fabrics and imagining what it would be like to wear the costumes.

'Now, ma petite,' said Madame Coco.

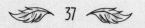

'Come and talk to me. I sense that
something is troubling you. Just wait one
moment and I make you a warm drink.'
She sat Alana down in a pink velvet
armchair and bustled off, returning with
some hot, sweet mint tea in a flowery
china tea cup.

'Now,' she said. 'Tell Madame Coco
what is the matter.' Alana looked at
Madame Coco's sympathetic face,
and suddenly she felt like telling her
everything. Her words pouring out in a
torrent, she told her all about her mum
working so hard and how she had to look

after her sister; about how she couldn't get the samba steps right and maybe she'd have to give up dancing. 'AND,' she continued, talking faster and faster, 'Mum was meant to make me a dress for the Latin Spectacular and she forgot and we can't afford a new one and I'm going to have to dance in an old skirt and leotard and Verity's dress is orange and gold and it's not fair and and . . . and . . .'

Madame Coco put up her hand for silence. 'You don't have a costume for the show, you say? Now *that*, ma petite, can be easily fixed!' She swept across the shop, flicked expertly between the dresses on one of the rails, and brought out the most amazing samba dress Alana had ever seen. It was a deep crimson, and covered with sequins and real diamonds!'

'Oh, it's beautiful,' Alana exclaimed. 'But I could never, *ever* afford it.'

'Well, ma petite, sometimes the right dress is just meant to be,' replied Madame Coco. 'Why don't you try it on?' She pointed to a corner of the room that was curtained off to make a fitting room. Alana went inside, and found the room was much bigger than it had looked on the outside. It was lined with mirrors, each one surrounded by light bulbs, just like in a theatre dressing room.

Alana slipped the dress over her head
and the skirts swirled around her hips
and legs. It felt like it had been made
just for her. Then she went back into
the main part of the shop to show it to
Madame Coco.

'Hmmm, very nice,' said Madame
Coco, looking at her approvingly.
'And these would go perfectly with it, I
think,' she added, taking a pair of dance
shoes off the shelf. They were made of
black patent leather with low heels and
sparkling diamanté buckles across the
front. To Alana's surprise, they fitted
beautifully. How could Madame Coco
have known my shoe size? she wondered.

'Why don't you try out your samba
routine?' asked Madame Coco.

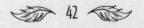

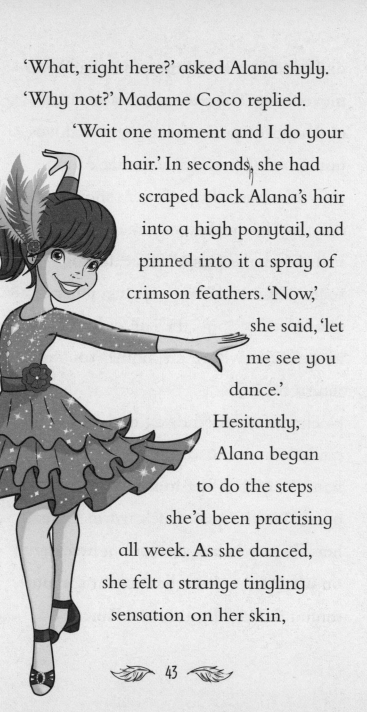

'What, right here?' asked Alana shyly.

'Why not?' Madame Coco replied.

'Wait one moment and I do your
hair.' In seconds, she had
scraped back Alana's hair
into a high ponytail, and
pinned into it a spray of
crimson feathers. 'Now,'
she said, 'let
me see you
dance.'
Hesitantly,
Alana began
to do the steps
she'd been practising
all week. As she danced,
she felt a strange tingling
sensation on her skin,

and her feet felt lighter and began to move faster. Then the ground seemed to disappear underneath her. *What* was going on? Trying not to panic, Alana closed her eyes, but still her feet kept dancing. In the distance, she could still hear Madame Coco's voice. It was saying, 'Remember, ma petite, when your good deed is done, the call of home will beckon. You will return home! You will return home!'

The voice faded away and all she could hear was a rushing sound like the wind. Then her feet touched the ground again, but this time it felt warm beneath her. There was hot sunshine, a breeze on her face, and the beat of drums and samba music filling the air. When she

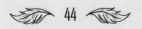

opened her eyes, she was still dancing the
samba, but she was on a road next to a
golden beach, with thousands of other
people who were dancing too!

Chapter 5

As Alana looked around her in amazement, she saw a large banner stuck into the sand, saying *Carnaval do Rio*. Was it possible? Was she really in Brazil, at the Rio Carnival? It had been early evening when she went into the shop, but now the sun was high in the sky.

Before she had time to wonder any more, a boy of about twelve with black curly hair and big dark eyes grabbed her

by the hand. 'Come on!' he said, and
he led her in the samba down the wide
road, expertly avoiding the other dancers.
It was as though she'd been doing the
dance all her life. The steps came easily,
and as she moved, her worries seemed to
fly away.

The band finished playing and the
boy led her across to a beach café where
he bought her some mango juice and
a chocolate ice cream. 'I am Carlos!'
he said, smiling. 'I saw that you were
dancing alone, and I just had to dance
with you.' Carlos was speaking a foreign
language – Portuguese it must be, Alana
thought, remembering when they'd
learned about Brazil at school. And yet,
strangely, she was able to understand him

perfectly. It was bizarre.

She blushed, but she didn't know what
to say so she just drank her juice. Luckily,
Carlos talked enough for both of them.
He told her that he was a member of a
local samba school and that the Carnival
was his favourite time of year. That
afternoon he was going to be performing
with his samba school in the parade.

Dancing was Carlos's life and he

wanted to do it professionally. But his papa had told him that he would have to leave his samba school after this year's Carnival, because he needed to spend more time studying. Papa wanted Carlos to become a doctor; dancing was all very well for fun, he thought, but it was not a career to be proud of.

Alana nodded and smiled as Carlos talked. When occasionally she made a comment, she found that she was speaking his language. She thought the words in English, but they came out in Portuguese! Was this magic?

Just then, a middle-aged man with a black moustache and a cross expression came hurrying up, gesturing angrily. 'There you are, Carlos!' he said. 'Why

aren't you doing your homework? Come home at once!'

'Papa, this is my new friend from England,' interrupted Carlos. His father looked a bit less stern as he turned and saw Alana. 'Can we invite her for lunch, Papa, please?'

'Yes, you may,' said Papa. 'But right now you must come home and study, you understand?'

'But, Papa,' said Carlos, 'I have to go to samba school for the final rehearsal before the parade, remember?'

'Ah, this samba, it is a waste of your time,' said Papa. 'But go! After today, you will be concentrating on more important matters.' Waving his hands, he shooed Carlos and Alana away.

Carlos took Alana's hand again. 'Never mind Papa,' he said. 'I am going to enjoy my last Carnival parade. Why don't you come with me to the samba school and watch our rehearsal?'

'I'd love to,' said Alana.

The school was only a short walk away, just off the beach. Once they'd stepped inside, Alana looked around in awe. The space was like Step Out Studio, but much, much bigger — and it was completely packed with dancers in the most fantastically elaborate and colourful costumes Alana had ever seen.

Carlos disappeared to change, leaving her sitting at the side of the room. As she began to get used to her surroundings, she realised there was only a small number of

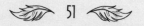

different costumes, with large numbers of dancers wearing each style. After a few minutes, Carlos came to join her wearing his costume, which was made of bright orange silk, with a pattern of flames licking all over it. On his head was an enormous headdress, with flame-like feathers standing out from it in vibrant red, orange and yellow. 'Every samba school must have a theme,' he explained. 'And this year, our theme is "fire".'

As he spoke, a tall woman in shorts and a T-shirt blew a whistle, and said something into a microphone. Alana

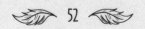

couldn't
hear what it
was. 'I must go,' said
Carlos. 'It is my group's
turn to rehearse.'

He went to join around a hundred other
dancers, all wearing orange fire costumes

identical to his. They got into position, as though in the parade, and as soon as the fast-paced samba music began, they were off – their feet moving exactly in time with each other. Alana tapped her foot and moved her hips, longing to join in.

As soon as Carlos's group had finished rehearsing, a different set of dancers began and Carlos joined Alana again. 'I'll go and change my clothes,' he said. 'Then it will be time to go home for lunch. After that, the real parade will begin!'

They walked through bustling streets to Carlos's house. The Carnival atmosphere was in the air and there was a feeling of excitement everywhere.

When they entered the house, Carlos's mother was busy in the kitchen, stirring

something in a huge cooking pot.
Delicious smells drifted through the
house. Carlos's mother was plump and
welcoming; she gave Alana a big hug
before carrying on with her cooking.

'Follow me! I'll show you round,'
said Carlos. His house was messy and
chaotic like Alana's own, but it was
filled with vibrant colours. In particular,
Alana noticed a wall-hanging covered in
intricate patterns. Looking more closely,
she realised that it was actually a large
flag, attached to a long pole.

'Ah yes,' said Carlos's papa when he
saw her looking at it. 'That wall-hanging
is very special to our family. It is a
banner made from the family emblems of
all our ancestors. I think of it as a badge

55

of our family pride. We are a very proud family indeed!'

Lunch at Carlos's house was incredible. They sat down with his three little brothers and sisters, his mother and father and grandmother, uncle, auntie and two cousins. Alana had never eaten food like this. There were tiny pastries stuffed with cheese and others filled with spicy meat; there were crisp corn cakes, and, for pudding, fried bananas and delicious chocolate truffles, which Carlos said

were called *brigadeiro*. Everyone talked and talked and ate and ate. Alana felt so comfortable and welcome that she chatted away, too.

Most of the talk was about the Carnival, of course. Everyone was so excited about the procession that afternoon. Alana kept glancing across at Carlos, and saw that his eyes were sad, because this was the last time he would be allowed to take part. He talked and ate with everyone else, but you could see his mind was elsewhere.

After lunch he disappeared upstairs to change back into his fire costume. As Alana was helping to clear the table, her eye kept being drawn to the family banner, that represented all the achievements of Carlos's ancestors. Poor Carlos, she

thought. It's not fair that he isn't allowed to follow his dream. If he loves to dance, surely his success would be the best way to make his family proud of him. I wish there was something I could do to help – but there isn't, is there?

As she was thinking, Carlos came back down. 'Come,' he said. 'It is time for the parade.' The sounds of samba bands were starting to drift through the open window and Carlos's little brothers and sisters dashed off to get a good position to watch the approaching spectacle.

Suddenly Alana had a brilliant idea. Checking that Papa was not in the room, she pulled the family banner down from the wall.

'What are you doing?' asked Carlos in

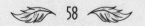

horror. 'Papa will go crazy!'

'Shhh – come on. Trust me!' said Alana, and taking him by the hand, she dragged him outside into the back streets of Rio, grasping the flag tightly.

But Carlos's father had noticed them leave, and with a cry of rage, he started to chase after them. With Carlos in his giant fiery headdress, it was not hard to spot them!

'Run!' cried Alana to Carlos.

'You're insane!' Carlos shouted, but he started running after her anyway. They slipped down a side alley, and when Alana glanced behind her, Papa was no longer there.

It was easy to find the parade – they just had to follow the beat of the music and the noise of singing and clapping from the crowd. Still, nothing could have prepared Alana for the scene that met her eyes as they entered the main boulevard. The broad avenue was packed from side to side with hundreds and hundreds of dancers and musicians. Each set of dancers wore matching outfits, and each seemed to be dressed more extravagantly than the last. There were sequins and glitter, jewels and feathers, enormous headdresses and killer heels. And the dancers moved in one rhythmic mass, with swinging hips and outstretched arms. Banked up on either side of the boulevard were rows of seats crammed with cheering onlookers.

They spotted the dancers from Carlos's samba school, waiting to take their place in the procession. Alana thrust the banner into Carlos's hands. 'You must wave this as you dance,' she shouted above the music.

Their dance began, and Carlos pulled Alana into the procession with him. He waved the banner high in the air, and as it flew in the breeze, different emblems shone brightly in the dazzling sunlight. Alana and Carlos turned to one side, and there was Papa at the front of the stands, shouting and shaking his fist.

'Look, Papa!' shouted Carlos,

straining to be heard above the noise of the samba drums. He waved the banner frantically. 'I'm dancing for the family, Papa! I'm dancing to make you proud of me!'

Carlos's voice was completely lost in all the background noise. But as Papa watched him dancing, waving the banner in the sunlight, he realised what Carlos was trying to do. His eyes that had been flashing with rage grew gentle, and he began to smile with pride.

As Alana and Carlos drew level with Papa, Carlos broke away from the dance for a moment to speak to him.

'Do you see, Papa?' said Carlos. 'Do you see that if you let me dance I can make my family proud?'

'Yes, I do see, my son,' said Papa, embracing him.

'So I will dance at the Carnival again? You will let me stay at samba school?'

'Yes,' said Papa. 'Yes, I will.'

Carlos pulled Alana back into the dance, his face alight with joy. The samba beat was growing faster and faster and Alana managed every move. Not only could she do the steps from the routine she'd learned for the Latin Spectacular, but she found she could dance all sorts of more complicated steps like the *corta jaca* and *batucada* as well. Her flame-coloured dress blended in beautifully, so she didn't look out of place at all.

As she spun around, she felt Carlos slip something into the hem at the back of

her dress. He whispered in her ear, 'Thank you, Alana. You have made us all so happy. Thank you.'

Then as if from far away, Alana could hear Madame Coco's voice. 'Remember, ma petite, when your good deed is done, the call of home will beckon. You will return home! You will return home!'

Alana closed her eyes but kept dancing. The sounds of the samba music gradually began to fade away. Again the ground seemed to disappear beneath her and she felt the rushing of a warm wind. When her feet touched the ground again, the floor felt hard and her steps echoed as though she were in a room instead of outside in the street.

Alana opened her eyes, and there she

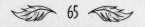

was back in Madame Coco's Costume Emporium. Madame Coco was sitting there just as she had been before, smiling pleasantly at Alana as though nothing out of the ordinary had happened. Alana found it hard to believe that the last few hours had been real. Apart from the fact that she was rather out of breath, nothing seemed to have changed. And when she looked over at the tall, dusty grandfather clock standing in the corner of the shop, she grew even more certain that she'd imagined it all. When she'd come into the shop it was five o'clock, and now the clock read a quarter past. She'd only got there fifteen minutes ago!

'I have to leave straight away,' said Alana. 'My mother will be waiting for me.

Thank you for letting me try on the dress, though. It's absolutely beautiful.'

'Why don't you keep it, ma petite?' replied Madame Coco. 'I think you have earned it today.'

'Oh but I couldn't,' said Alana, stroking the sparkling material longingly. 'It's far too expensive.'

'Take it, ma chérie,' said Madame Coco, zipping it carefully inside a dress cover. 'It is meant for you.'

Alana threw her arms round Madame Coco, whooping with joy. 'Thank you thank you!' she said. 'If I could borrow it for a day or two, that is all I want.'

'It is nothing,' said Madame Coco, looking a bit embarrassed. 'And wait – you must take this as well.' Madame Coco

handed Alana a beautiful album covered in
purple brocade interwoven with gold threads.
It had thick, cream-coloured paper inside,
and lots of empty pockets to put things in.

Alana thanked Madame Coco again,
then she left the shop and ran down the
street to her front door, the dress hidden
under her coat.

As she let herself in, her mother seemed
to be looking guilty, as though she were
trying to hide something from Alana.

'Whatever,' thought Alana. 'I've got enough things to think about without worrying about what Mum is up to.' Alana did not want to tell anyone about the dress just yet.

She ran up to her room and hung the beautiful dress carefully in her wardrobe. There were so many layers of skirts that she had trouble shutting the door!

She was keen to get an early night before the show the next day, so she went upstairs straight after supper and got ready for bed. As she drifted off to sleep, she felt much more confident about the Spectacular than she would have imagined possible a few hours earlier. She felt sure she'd manage the steps now – *and* she had a fabulous dress!

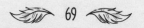

Chapter 6

The next day was Saturday – the day of
the Latin Spectacular. As soon as she'd
finished breakfast, Alana dashed round to
Meena's house to hang out and maybe
try some last-minute practice. They didn't
have to be at the theatre until after lunch.

The girls went up to Meena's room
to chat. Meena put on TJS's latest song,
then they settled down to paint their nails
for the show. Alana picked out a clear

nail varnish that had tiny silver stars in it, and Meena decided on a cobalt blue that exactly matched her samba dress. As they brushed on the varnish, the smell of roasting chapattis wafted up the stairs. Alana couldn't wait for lunch. Meena's grandma did most of the cooking in her house, and meals were always pretty special.

'I hope it's going to go OK this afternoon,' Meena sighed.

'Me too,' said Alana. 'Even if I get my steps right, Toby might mess up. He could be a good dancer if he wanted to, but he doesn't even try.'

'I know,' said Meena, 'but it's not really his fault, seeing as he doesn't even want to go to dance classes. His mum should

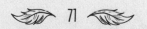

listen to what *he* wants to do, not what *she* wants him to do. Just cos she couldn't be a dancer herself. It's not fair.'

'You like Toby, don't you!' said Alana teasingly.

'He's OK,' said Meena, blushing. 'But that's not the point. I just think he has a hard time, that's all.'

After lunch, it was time to set off to the theatre. Meena's mum dropped them off at the stage door in the car. They made their way through  the backstage area, carrying their dresses carefully over one arm. When they got to the dressing room, they were impressed to see a printed sign saying 'Students of Step Out Studio' on the door. Inside, everything was a whirl, with far too many students crammed into too small a space, putting up their hair, doing their make-up and talking non-stop.

As Alana began to get ready, her mind floated back to Madame Coco's Costume Emporium. Just who was Madame Coco, and where did her shop come from, and why did she want to help Alana? It was all such a mystery.

'What are you dreaming about?' asked Meena as she put on her stage make-up.

'She's probably dreaming she had a mother who could buy her a proper dress for the Spectacular,' chipped in Verity,

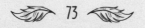

laughing unpleasantly. Verity, who had just arrived, was dressed from head to toe in designer clothes and was carrying a double skinny latte.

'Actually,' said Alana with her sweetest smile, 'this is my dress, here.' She unzipped the cover of Madame Coco's costume.

Verity looked at the stunning dress. Layer upon layer of skirts floated out, each one studded with gold sequins. Hundreds of diamonds glittered on the bodice, dazzling in the bright dressing-room lights.

For a moment, Verity's face was nearly as crimson as the dress, but then she got herself under control. 'You don't imagine anyone will think those diamonds are real, do you?' she asked,

with a mean laugh, and she glided off to
practise her steps.

'Just ignore her,' whispered Meena.
'Who cares if the diamonds aren't real?
The dress is absolutely beautiful.'

Alana could hardly tell her that,
actually, they *were* real! 'Come on,' she

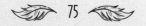

said, 'let's go and work on the dance.'

They walked on to the stage where lots of other dancers were busy practising, and Alana felt a flutter of nervousness as she looked out into the empty auditorium. Soon those seats would be filled with people expecting to be entertained. Would she be able to achieve this or would she struggle to remember her steps, just like she had done in rehearsal?

But as Alana and Meena began to work through the samba routine, Alana practically forgot where she was. The theatre seemed to fade away and she could almost smell the hot smells of the Carnival again, hear the beat of the drums and feel the excitement of the dance pulsing through her. It's so weird, she thought. Rio must have been just a dream, but it's the most real dream I've ever had.

She was brought sharply back to reality by a high-pitched scream from the dressing rooms. She recognised Chloe's voice immediately.

'Oh no, what do you think has happened to Chloe?' asked Meena.

'We'd better go and see,' Alana replied, and they hurried towards the sound.

As the girls got closer, they could hear Verity's voice in between Chloe's shrieks. They heard the word 'dress . . .' and 'all spoiled . . .' and then, 'Alana'. Alana's stomach seemed to flip over, and she started to run.

When she entered the dressing room,

the first thing she saw was her dress, hanging on its peg. Right down the front of it was an ugly coffee stain. The coffee was still drip-drip-dripping, making a puddle on the floor below it. Chloe, red-faced and crying, was dabbing at the dress with a towel. 'Oh poor, poor Alana,'

she was wailing, 'her lovely dress!'

Alana was so shocked she couldn't even move. What on earth was Madame Coco going to say when she found out her beautiful dress was spoiled?

Verity was sitting nearby, her long legs crossed, her lips curled upwards in a pleased smirk. When she saw Alana, the smirk transformed into a grin. 'I'm terribly sorry, Alana,' she said in a fake voice, 'but Chloe has spilled coffee all over your dress. It's completely ruined, I'm afraid.'

'I didn't do it, honestly,' sobbed Chloe.

'It's all right, Chloe,' Alana said quietly, putting her arm round her. 'If you say it wasn't you, I believe you.'

In fact, Alana had a very strong idea

who had actually ruined her costume. Verity was looking far too pleased with herself. Alana gently took the towel away from Chloe. 'Don't worry about trying to clean the dress – it won't do any good.' Slowly, Chloe's sobs subsided.

Just then, the door opened and there was Miss Trina. She looked shocked as she took in the scene: the dress hanging ruined, Chloe looking wretched, Alana trying not to cry with Meena comforting her, and Verity sitting there, smugly. She grasped what must have happened in a moment. But there was no time to do anything about it. As everyone tried to talk at once, she held up a hand for silence.

'I'll sort this out later, girls,' she said.

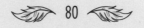

'Alana, your mother is here and she
needs to speak to you. She says it's
urgent. Off you go.'

What can it be now? thought Alana
as she ran to the stage door. Could the
day get any worse? First her dress was
spoiled, and now her mum was here with
some emergency or other. Surely she
wasn't going to expect her to look after
Abi today of all days. Even without a
dress, Alana couldn't bear the thought of
missing the show!

But when Alana saw her Mum, she
looked excited, not worried and stressed.
She was carrying a large plastic bag.

'Hi, love,' she said, giving Alana a kiss
on the cheek. 'You know, I felt awful
about what I said to you yesterday,

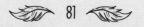

about giving up dancing. I know how much it means to you. And I felt guilty for forgetting to make your dress as well. So I stayed up all night, and I persuaded my boss to give me the day off work to finish it — and here it is.' And she drew out of the plastic bag a gorgeous samba dress, made from the sea-green material that she and Alana had bought together the week before. It wasn't perfect — you could tell it had been made in a hurry, because the stitches were rather large and there were some loose threads here and there. But she had bought some special green sequins to sew on to the skirts and it was obvious she'd made a real effort.

Alana loved it. 'It's fabulous, Mum!

Thank you!' she said, throwing her arms around her and giving her a huge hug. The dress may not have been as fancy as the one that Madame Coco had given her, but her mum had made it, and that meant it was much more precious to her.

'And, seeing as I've managed to get the day off,' said Mum, 'Abi and I can come to the show. We can't wait to see you dance the samba!'

Now I really will have to do a great
job, thought Alana, as she dashed back to
the dressing room to try on the new dress.

'What's that?' asked Verity sharply,
when she saw Alana walk in with the sea-
green costume glittering over her arm.

'Oh, just another dress,' said Alana
airily. 'I'm quite glad the other one got
spoiled, actually, because I think I look
better in green.'

Verity's face turned a pale shade of
green to match.

Chapter 7

As the audience started to file into the
theatre, the Step Out Studio students kept
peeping round the stage curtain to watch
the audience arriving. In came Verity's
parents, her dad in a posh suit and her
mum in a real fur coat; Toby's mum,
looking concerned, and fiddling with her
programme; Meena's mum and granny,
trying to control her little brother and
sister who were arguing about where to

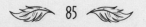

sit . . . and Chloe was there, too, sitting in the front row. She'd only just started at Step Out Studio so she hadn't had time to learn the routine for the show. She was keen to watch, though, even if she couldn't join in this time around.

Alana started to feel nervous – the seats were nearly all taken and the curtain was going up in five minutes. Where were Mum and Abi? Then she saw the two of them dashing through the door, her mum looking flustered, Abi looking excited. Alana breathed a big sigh.

Everyone else was waiting in the wings now because the show was about to start. Alana went to join them.

'I hope you're not going to let us all down, Alana,' said Verity. 'The way you

were dancing at rehearsal, I shouldn't think Miss Trina will want you at Step Out Studio after today.'

'Just ignore her!' said Meena, fiercely, squeezing Alana's arm.

In fact, Alana had no trouble ignoring Verity, because she just felt in her bones that everything was going to go OK.

The band struck up, playing Alana's favourite samba music with its quick syncopated beat. Immediately the theatre seemed to vibrate with a hot Carnival atmosphere.

'Get ready for your cue, everyone!' said Miss Trina.

As the students danced on to the stage in an explosion of rhythm and energy, there was a huge round of applause. Alana danced the steps perfectly, without even thinking about it, and Toby rose to the occasion, partnering her effortlessly. Then, towards the end of the dance when they were meant to repeat the first section, Alana found herself doing an amazing new routine. It was far more complicated than anything the students

had been taught
by Miss Trina, but
Alana danced as
if she'd been doing
it all her life.

The audience
started to cheer,
and looking
up, Alana
caught her
mum's eye. In
her face she could
see the same look
that she'd seen in
Carlos's papa's —
pride and joy at watching her child doing
what she loved best.

When the dance was finished and

the students had taken their bows, the audience started up a chant of 'Alana! Alana!' and she had to come back on stage and take an extra bow all by herself. When the curtain fell for the last time, the other students crowded round her to congratulate her.

'Wow, that was unbelievable, Alana,' said Meena. How did you learn to do that since Thursday?'

'Oooh,' said Chloe, who'd come backstage to join the others. 'You were fabulous! I wish I could dance like you!'

Even Toby made a comment. 'You were cool,' he said, a bit grudgingly.

Then Miss Trina came up to her. She'd been busy chatting to the students' families. 'Wow, Alana – you blew me

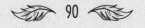

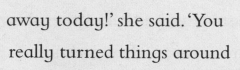

away today!' she said. 'You really turned things around since rehearsal. You must have been practising hard!'

Alana smiled, but she didn't say anything.

Only Verity didn't look pleased. Alana spotted her backstage with her parents. Her lips were pinched and her eyes glinted with malice. 'Did you *see* that girl Alana showing off?' she was saying to her mother, not bothering to lower her voice. 'It was *so* embarrassing.'

'Yes, princess. It was *extremely* vulgar. I don't know what Miss Trina is thinking letting a girl like that dance at Step Out Studio.'

'And what about her dress?' continued Verity. 'The stitches were so big I expect you could see them from where you were sitting!'

Alana walked away before she had to listen any more. She didn't much care anyway. Somehow, Verity didn't seem to be making herself feel any better by being nasty about her – the more she talked, the more furious she looked!

Chapter 8

When they got home, Alana's mum cooked up her favourite meal: pizza with mushrooms and extra cheese, and garlic bread.

'Yum yum!' said Abi, as they ate pots of chocolate mousse for pudding. 'Alana, can you be in a dance show every day?'

'Please no!' said mum holding her head in her hands. 'I couldn't stand the stress!'

After supper, Alana was in such a good

mood that she didn't even mind that her mum had to spend the evening studying, leaving her to take care of her sister.

Alana got Abi in the bath and made her brush her teeth. Abi couldn't stop talking about the show. 'You were so great!' she said, bouncing up and down instead of getting into her pyjamas. 'I can't wait to

tell all my friends at school about it!'

When Alana had managed to get Abi tucked up in bed at last, she went into her own room and closed the door, glad to be alone.

She lay down on her bed, her thoughts in a whirl as she went over everything that had happened since yesterday. Even if Rio had just been a dream, *what* a dream it was! *And* she had found a new friend in Madame Coco and discovered her extraordinary shop. *And* her mum had realised how important dancing was to her – for now at least. *And* she'd performed brilliantly in the show!

Alana got up to put away the two samba costumes – the one her mum had made her and the one Madame Coco

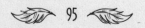

had lent her. But as she was hanging up Madame Coco's dress, she looked at in amazement. 'How bizarre,' she thought. 'The coffee stain has gone!' It didn't make any sense. She hadn't even had a chance even to try to get it off.

Alana sighed with relief. Now, when she returned the dress to Madame Coco, she wouldn't have to explain why it was covered in coffee.

Just as she was closing the wardrobe door again, something green and yellow caught her eye, sticking up from the hem of the dress. She drew it out gently and saw that it was a small Brazilian flag, beautifully embroidered.

'Wait a minute!' she thought. 'I remember seeing this patch on Carlos's

banner! *And* I remember
feeling him slipping
something into the hem of
my dress before I left him! So it *was* all
real – it *must* have been! The Carnival, the
beach, the sunshine; Carlos's family, the

parade . . . it actually happened!'

Suddenly, she knew why Madame Coco had given her the purple and gold album. Opening it carefully, she stuck the little flag on to the first page. Then getting out her best gold and silver gel pens, she made a swirly pattern all around it.

As she lay in bed that night, she stared at the album on her shelf. 'There are lots of pages in it,' she thought to herself. 'Does that mean Madame Coco thinks I'm going to have lots of adventures, so I can fill the pages with more souvenirs?'

Alana slept deeply that night, dreaming about what costume she would try on next time she went to Madame Coco's Costume Emporium.

Enter
Arlene's World
of Dance . . .

Become a samba star!

Imagine you're dancing in Brazil, just like Alana and Carlos. These special moves should help you perfect a magical carnival samba!

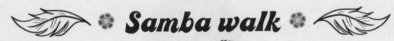

Samba walk

The samba walk is a bouncy step that uses the ball of the foot.

Volta

The volta is a good travelling step and
has a nice bounce action.

Roll

The samba roll is when partners' bodies are
close together and rotating.

Fantastic samba facts!

Samba is a lively, rhythmical dance
of Brazilian origin in 2/4 time danced
to samba music.

The Portuguese imported many slaves
from Africa into Brazil in the sixteenth
century, who in turn brought their
dances, including the samba.

The word 'samba' may come from
the common word in West African Bantu
languages meaning to pray, or to
invoke the spirits of the gods.

The samba is meant to be a dance that excites people and brings people into a sort of trance.

Gradually members of the upper classes in Rio embraced the dance and it was incorporated into their ballroom tradition.

Now considered one of the most popular Brazilian cultural expressions, the samba has become an icon of Brazilian national identity and it is danced at the Rio Carnival every year.

Take a step further with Alana on her dancing adventures...

Collect all these fabulous stories!

Out now!

Book 2: LA Moves

Alana and best friend Meena are practising a dance for the School Review. But their classmates think it's boring. What are they going to do?

Madame Coco's Costume Emporium has just the thing to help! When Alana tries on a magical dance outfit, she finds herself in America performing street dance with hot boy band TJS!

Will she be able to make her School Review sizzle with superstar excitement?

Coming out January 2011!

Book 3: A Viennese Waltz

Alana is getting ready for the Ballroom Bonanza
competition in London. But mum needs her to spend
all her time babysitting, and now she's lost her
partner.

Madame Coco has just the solution – a beautiful
gown that magically transports her to the royal
ballrooms of Vienna. Will Alana be able to dance
with a prince and make it back to waltz her way to
brilliance in the Ballroom Bonanza?

Book 4: Bollywood Dreams

Alana wants to help her best friend Meena
audition for a brand new show, Bollywood Dreams.
They both love Bollywood films, but they're not sure
they've got the steps quite right.

Madame Coco knows just what to do! It's one
short trip to her Costume Emporium before Alana
is magically whisked off to the set of a fabulous new
Bollywood film, dancing with beautiful movies stars
and learning all the best steps to help make
Meena a star too.

Coming out May 2011!

Book 5: Stage Sensation

Alana and her friends from Step Out Studio
are gearing up for a new performance in a show-
stopping musical. They all want to sing and dance
on stage, but some of them are finding the new
routines really hard.

Madame Coco's is the place to go! There, Alana is
transported to the bright lights of Broadway in New
York City where she meets the members of an amazing
dance troupe. Can she learn how to dazzle on stage
and help her friends become musical superstars?

Book 6: Twilight Tango

Alana faces her most difficult challenge yet – to
master the tricky tango. As she and her friends at
Step Out Studio struggle with the complicated
moves, their new show is suddenly put in jeopardy.

Madame Coco knows just what will help. Putting
on one of her stunning tango costumes, Alana is
magically whisked away to the backstreets of Buenos
Aires in Argentina where she is taught the passionate
story of the tango. Can she take all she has learned
back home to help her friends
dance a thrilling tango?